SHIP'S COOK GINGER

ANOTHER TIM STORY

by

Edward Ardizzone

Macmillan Publishing Co., Inc.
New York

Macmillan Publishing Co., Inc.
866 Third Avenue, New York, N.Y. 10022
First American edition 1978
Printed in the United States of America
10   9   8   7   6   5   4   3   2   1

LIBRARY OF CONGRESS CATALOGING IN PUBLICATION DATA
Ardizzone, Edward, *date*
Ship's cook Ginger.
SUMMARY: Two boys who work and live with
a ship's crew during a voyage to the Northern
Isles are assigned extra duties when the captain
and half the crew become ill.
[1. Sea stories] I. Title.
PZ7.A682Sh 1978   [E]   78-7518   ISBN 0-02-705680-5

It was holiday time and Tim and Ginger, who lived by the sea, were bored.

There was no one on the beach to play with and not even the old boatman to talk to.

'Let's run away to sea again,' said Ginger crossly, but Tim said that he couldn't because he had promised his mother not to.

'Oh, poof! You and your silly old promises,' shouted Ginger more crossly than before.

Tim's mother noticed that Tim looked pale, mooched about and would not finish his dinner, so she went to the chemist and bought a big bottle of tonic. The chemist said it was the best tonic he had. It was especially good for boys because it was so nasty that they hurried up and became better.

And, my word, it was nasty. Poor Tim had to take three large spoonfuls of it a day.

But in spite of this he mooched about more and more, became paler and paler, ate less and less of his dinner and even began to get thinner.

Tim's father said that he knew what was wrong with Tim, that tonics would not help. The boy was pining for the open sea.

Why not ask Captain McFee to take them all for a voyage in his new ship? Ginger of course must come too.

Tim's mother did not like the idea at all. Something horrid always happened when Tim and Ginger went to sea. Tim's father said, 'Nonsense, my dear. This time we will be with them which makes all the difference.' But Tim's mother was still worried and she was right.

The next day they walked to the docks where they found Captain McFee in his ship *Claribel*.

Captain McFee said that he was sailing in three days' time for the Northern Isles and would be pleased to take them with him. He had a nice cabin for Tim's father and mother, but the boys would have to work and live with the crew.

You can just imagine how excited were Tim and Ginger as they packed and helped to get everything ready for the voyage. The only person who sometimes looked sad was Tim's mother.

The cat was sad too because he was going to be left behind.

However, when they arrived on board the *Claribel* and Tim's mother saw their cabin she felt much happier. It was beautiful.

Tim's job was to stay on the bridge and help the Captain by doing such things as running messages and fetching the Captain his tea.

Ginger, who was not so clever, had to help the second mate. He had to paint and scrub and do other kinds of work.

Unfortunately he was sometimes idle and would hide in a boat and read comics instead of getting on with the job. This made him unpopular with the second mate who did not like boys anyhow and who was often nasty to him.

For the first few days the weather was lovely. The sky was blue, the sea was blue and the little waves danced and sparkled in the sun.

Tim's father and mother sat in deck chairs in the sun and were having a lovely restful holiday.

Tim enjoyed working for the Captain and even Ginger did not mind scrubbing decks in the nice bright warm weather.

Best of all the ship's cook was a very good cook and made the most scrumptious meat pies.

THEN THE BLOW FELL...

One day Sparks the wireless officer asked Tim to take a message to his father.

When his father read it he was horrified. 'Something dreadful has happened at the office,' he said. 'We must all go home at once or we will be ruined.'

Captain McFee was very kind and said that he would put them on shore at the nearest port where they could get a train home, but he would like the boys to stay with him as he found them very useful. Tim's mother did not like this a bit and said 'NO'.

Tim and Ginger begged and begged her to let them stay. At last she said yes, though she was very unhappy about it.

The Captain gave Tim and Ginger leave to go to the station and see Tim's parents off, but he said that they must be back on board by nine o'clock as the *Claribel* sailed then. This left plenty

of time for the boys to have a lovely meal of fish and chips, with ices to follow.

In fact, when they arrived on board they were too full to eat even a tiny bit of the cook's scrumptious meat pie, which, as you will find out later, was lucky for them.

When Tim went up to the bridge next morning he was happy to find that the *Claribel* was now at sea and out of sight of land, but he was unhappy to find the Captain looking ill and the man at the wheel not much better.

All the Captain could say was, 'Get me some tea. I feel awful.'

Tim dashed down to the galley. There he found the cook lying on the floor. When the cook saw Tim he gave a groan and said, 'Don't eat the pie,' and fainted away.

Then Tim ran to the wireless cabin to find Sparks also lying on the floor. Sparks whispered a message before he fainted.

Back on the bridge again Tim found the second mate standing by the wheel. Captain McFee had fainted away and the sailor was groaning on the deck.

'Boy,' said the second mate, 'the first mate is sick, as well as half the crew. I am now in command of this ship. We will wait here for a relief ship to take the sick to a hospital on shore. Then we will go on with the voyage. But remember we now have only half a crew, so you boys will have to work twice as hard.

'Ginger tells me he is a good cook, so I have made him ship's cook.'

By the time the relief ship had arrived, the wind blew harder and the waves were too big for the ships to float side by side, so the sick men had to be taken to the relief ship in boats; a long and dangerous task.

Tim's job was to look after the sick men as his boat went backwards and forwards between the ships. Ginger was kept in the galley cooking a hot meal for tired men.

And the crew of the *Claribel* were indeed tired
as they settled down to what they hoped would
be a lovely hot meal. But it was horrible. It was
a stew and the bosun found a mouse in his
portion. Ginger was very unpopular.

Poor Tim, like all the others, could not eat his stew and was so hungry and so tired that he longed to go to sleep in his bunk. But this was not to be. The second mate called for him to go to the bridge.

The engines had now been started and the ship moved forward in the teeth of a gale. Big waves and driving rain made it difficult to see ahead.

The mate ordered Tim to take the wheel from Seaman Bloggs who was tired, and to steer North and keep a sharp lookout.

'But, sir,' said Tim, 'Captain McFee said we must steer East to avoid the Black Cape and its deadly rocks.'

'What!' roared the mate. 'Question my orders? Be off with you. I will deal with you in the morning.'

Sadly Tim crept into his bunk. He was frightened because he knew he was right.

Poor Tim could not sleep, he could only wonder how to save the ship and possibly their lives. At last he said to himself, 'I must tell the bosun.'

'You are right, my boy,' said the bosun. 'We should travel East but it is no good telling the mate, he would only be angry. We must have a plan, but we have some days to spare, so go to bed and sleep.'

The next few days were horrible for all. Ginger's cooking became worse than ever. He put, by mistake, sugar in the soup and salt in the custard. He even put mustard in the coffee to make it taste warmer and his sandwiches of bread and raspberry jam with a sardine in the middle were the nastiest of the lot.

Poor Tim had a horrible time too. As they were short of crew he had to spend many hours at the wheel. The bosun's plan was that Tim should steer to the East every time the mate was not looking, and if he was caught out to make excuses.

Excuses such as—

'There was a trawler on the port bow.'

'I had to avoid a whale.'

'A coastal steamer was passing in shore of us.'

But all the time Tim was worried because he was not sure that the mate believed him and, worse still, because he was not sure if he had steered the ship enough to the East to avoid the deadly rocks ahead.

The next morning he was to know.

It was early when Tim heard sailors shouting, 'Rocks ahead!' and rushed to the bridge. There he found the bosun and the mate.

Looking ahead he could just see the Black

Cape and a line of terrible rocks with waves
breaking over them.

The mate was too frightened to do anything
but tremble. The bosun took charge.

The bosun told Tim to take the wheel, while he went on deck to get the men to collect planks and ropes to make some sort of raft, should the worst happen and the *Claribel* get smashed on the rocks.

Tim did his best to steer clear of the rock he saw ahead, but it got nearer and nearer all the time. From outside he could hear the sound of the waves and of men shouting. From inside only the terrible chattering of the mate's teeth. He was shivering with fear.

Then the miracle happened. The *Claribel* had almost struck the rock when an extra big wave lifted her past it. The rock was the outermost rock so the *Claribel* was now safe in open water.

A great cheer came from the men on deck. Many ran up to the bridge to shake Tim's hand and cry out, 'You've saved us. Your steering has saved us.'

From here it was only a short way to the next port. Soon they were inside the little harbour. On the quay was Captain McFee and with him all the crew they had left behind. They were quite well now.

Once on board Captain McFee soon heard

about the *Claribel*'s narrow escape and asked the mate how it had happened. The mate said that it was all Tim's fault for not obeying his orders.

The Captain looked at Tim with a sad stern face, but poor Tim could say nothing. After all he had disobeyed orders, though it was to save the ship.

The bosun and some
of the crew standing
nearby heard what was
said and, not wanting
Tim to be blamed,
told the Captain
the whole story.

Is this true boy?

Yes Sir

Upon which the Captain turned on the mate in fury and called him—

> a liar
>
> a coward
>
> a poltroon
>
> a bad sailor

and lots of other horrible names and then dismissed him the ship.

On the voyage home the *Claribel* was a happy ship. The weather was fine, the old cook was back so the crew had delicious meals to eat, there were enough sailors on board so nobody had to work too hard, and the horrid second mate was not there to be beastly.

Captain McFee was particularly nice to Tim. He taught him how to guide a ship by the sun and stars and other things called the Art of Navigation.

The cook was rather sorry for Ginger and being
a kind man he arranged for Ginger to help him
in the galley.

There he taught Ginger how to roast meat,
make stews, cook vegetables, also make pastry
and lots of delicious puddings.

Ginger really worked hard, did not answer back and learnt to cook quite well. His scrumptious pies were nearly as good as the cook's.